Animales pequeñitos / Itty Bitty Animals

GUPPIES PEQUEÑITOS/ ITTY BITTY GUPPIES

By Alex Lumpy

Traducción al español: Eida de la Vega

Gareth Stevens
Publishing

Please visit our website, www.garethstevens.com. For a free color catalog of all our high-quality books, call toll free 1-800-542-2595 or fax 1-877-542-2596.

Library of Congress Cataloging-in-Publication Data

Lumpy, Alex.
Itty bitty guppies = *Guppies* pequeñitos / by Alex Lumpy.
 p. cm. — (Itty bitty animals = Animales pequeñitos)
Parallel title: *Guppies* pequeñitos
In English and Spanish
Includes index.
ISBN 978-1-4339-9907-9 (library binding)
1. Guppies — Juvenile literature. I. Title.
SF458.G8 L86 2014
639.3757—dc23

First Edition

Published in 2014 by
Gareth Stevens Publishing
111 East 14th Street, Suite 349
New York, NY 10003

Copyright © 2014 Gareth Stevens Publishing

Editor: Ryan Nagelhout
Designer: Nicholas Domiano
Spanish Translation: Eida de la Vega

Photo credits: Cover, pp. 1, 21, 24 (fry) Sailesh Patel/Shutterstock.com; p. 5 © iStockphoto.com/scottyspics; p. 7 Nikolay Dimitrov - ecobo/Shutterstock.com; p. 9 bluehand/Shutterstock.com; p. 11, 24 (stripe) Andrew Illyasov/E+/Getty Images; p. 13 subin pumsom/Shutterstock.com; p. 15 LDiza/Shutterstock.com; p. 17 Kerstin Klaassen/E+/Getty Images; p. 19 Richard Boll/Photographer's Choice/Getty Images; p. 23 Mijang Ka/Flickr/ Getty Images; p. 24 (water) iStockphoto/Thinkstock.com.

All rights reserved. No part of this book may be reproduced in any form without permission in writing from the publisher, except by a reviewer.

Printed in the United States of America

CPSIA compliance information: Batch #CW14GS: For further information contact Gareth Stevens, New York, New York at 1-800-542-2595.

Contenido

Guppies diminutos 4

Un gran descubrimiento .12

El día de los alevines 20

Palabras que debes saber 24

Índice 24

Contents

Tiny Guppies 4

Big Discovery 12

Fry Day 20

Words to Know 24

Index 24

¡Los *guppies*, o peces millón, son diminutos!

Guppies are little fish!

5

Les gusta nadar
en el agua.

They like to swim
in water.

7

Los *guppies* tienen muchos colores.

They are full of color.

9

Algunos tienen franjas.

Some have stripes.

11

Se descubrieron en 1866.

They were discovered in 1866.

13

Los *guppies* machos
son más pequeños
que las hembras.

Boy guppies are smaller
than girls.

15

Las hembras no ponen huevos. Dan a luz a bebés vivos.

Girl guppies do not lay eggs. They give birth to live babies.

17

¡Los *guppies* bebés pueden nadar enseguida que nacen!

Baby guppies can swim right away!

19

Un *guppy* bebé se llama alevín.

A baby guppy is called a fry.

21

Los *guppies* son buenas mascotas.

Guppies make great pets.

23

Palabras que debes saber/ Words to Know

(el) alevín/ fry

(las) franjas/ stripes

(el) agua/ water

Índice / Index

alevín/fry 20

bebés/babies 16, 18, 20

franjas/stripes 10

mascotas/pets 22